Not Your Mama, Not Your Milk

A Tale of Friendship, Compassion, and Freedom

By
B.A. DeLong

For my Penny,

My most loyal companion and truest friend.

In a serene, sun-dappled woodland on the outskirts of a small, peaceful town, three best friends—Rocco, Penny, and Sarge—gathered at their usual hangout spot in a cozy clearing surrounded by towering oaks and the cheerful hum of birdsong.

They were an unlikely trio. Rocco, a scrappy raccoon with boundless energy and a nose for adventure, was always the first to dive headfirst into something new. Penny, a sweet little bunny with a heart as big as her fluffy white tail, preferred splashing in the creek or offering a comforting nuzzle to anyone in need. Sarge, a thoughtful fox, was the steady voice of reason, carefully considering every plan before adding his measured approval.

"Let's go explore!" shouted Rocco, his tail wagging furiously as he darted to the edge of the clearing.

"I want to go swimming!" Penny chimed, already imagining the cool water on her fur, as she bounded toward the creek.

"Can we play hide and seek?" asked Sarge, his ears perking up at the thought of a quiet, strategic game.

The woodland seemed to shimmer with endless possibilities for fun and adventure. But before they could settle on a plan, a strange noise broke through the usual calm, rustling the leaves and pulling their attention in an unexpected direction, stopping them in their tracks.

Let's go explore!
I Want To Go Swimming!
Can we play hide and seek?

Through the trees, they spotted something running toward them from the direction of the old dairy farm down the road. Curious and alarmed, they dashed to the clearing to get a better look. As the figure drew closer, they realized it was an exhausted and distraught cow.

"Help... please," the cow whispered, her voice barely audible. Rocco immediately ran to her side, his tail low, his usual bravado replaced with concern.

"Are you okay? What happened?" Penny asked softly, stepping closer and lowering her head to meet the cow's gaze.

Sarge stayed a few steps back, scanning the direction she had come from with a watchful eye. "She looks like she's been running for miles," he murmured. "Something must have scared her pretty bad."

The cow tried to speak again, but her words were lost in a sobbing moo. Penny gently nudged her with her nose. "It's okay," she said soothingly. "Take your time. You're safe here."

The three friends shared a glance, silently agreeing to do whatever they could to help. Something about the way this cow looked—exhausted, terrified, and yet deter-mined—told them her story was far from ordinary.

Panting heavily, the cow introduced herself as McKenzie. She had run away from the dairy farm in a desperate attempt to chase a truck that had taken her newborn calf. Trembling and weak, McKenzie pleaded with Rocco, Penny, and Sarge to help her find her baby.

Sarge stood nearby, his ears alert, scanning the clearing for any signs of danger. "We'll figure this out," he said confidently. "We'll bring back answers. You have my word."

McKenzie's voice trembled with desperation as she tried to explain. "I chased that truck as far as I could, but I couldn't keep up, and I lost sight of it. I can't stop thinking about the sound of his tiny cries as they took him farther and farther away." Her voice broke, and she lowered her head in despair.

Penny gently rubbed McKenzie's forehead, her voice soft and soothing. "You're safe now," she murmured, pressing her nose gently against McKenzie's muzzle in reassurance.

Rocco paced a few steps, his mind churning with ideas. "We'll go to the farm to find out what's going on, we'll do everything we can to help get your baby back," he added with steady resolve. "You just focus on resting and getting your strength back."

Rocco, Penny, and Sarge felt their hearts ache for McKenzie. The trio quickly gathered soft leaves and grass to make a comfortable spot for her to rest while they were gone.

Rocco worked with determined focus, and Sarge stood watch, his keen eyes scanning the woods for any signs of danger.

"You don't have to go through this alone. You have us now," Penny whispered, her voice soft and full of kindness, before turning to follow the others toward the farm.

McKenzie blinked back tears, a flicker of hope lighting up her exhausted face. "Thank you," was all the reply she could muster in a heartfelt whisper as she watched them go.

Their short journey down the road led them to the old farm. As they approached the big red barn, the smell of hay and damp earth lingered in the air. Inside they found rows of mother cows confined to cramped stalls, and distressed moos echoed through the barn.

Rocco slowly approached a group of cows and asked, "Why do all of you look so tired and sad? Do you know a cow named McKenzie? Do you know anything about McKenzie's missing calf?"

One of the cows shook her head, tears in her eyes. "It happens to us all. The farmer takes our babies away so he can sell our milk. After we have given them as many babies as we can, they send us away too. We don't know where."

Penny's eyes welled with tears. "That's awful! Why would anyone do that?"

"We're just property to them," another cow murmured bitterly. "We have no say."

Shaken, the three friends promised the mother cows they would return with a plan.

As they left the barn, the sun felt harsher, and their hearts felt heavier. Rocco, Penny, and Sarge walked in silence, their paws brushing against the dry grass, their usual chatter replaced with troubling thoughts. They glanced back toward the barn, where the sad, pleading eyes of the mama cows seemed etched into their memory.

Rocco kicked a pebble along the path, frustration bubbling in his chest. Who would take a baby away from its mother? And why would anyone drink milk that came from someone else's mama?" he muttered, his words sharp with anger. He couldn't understand it.

Sarge, usually the calm and collected one, sighed deeply. His ears drooped slightly as he stared at the ground. "And where do the older cows go when they can't make milk anymore?" he asked softly. "And what about the newborn calves? Where do they take them?"

"We have to do something," Penny whispered, as they reached their hangout spot. Her voice carried a mix of sadness and resolve. "If we don't, who will?"

Rocco nodded, his usual boldness returning in a flicker. "We'll figure it out," he said firmly, his tail swishing with de-termination. "For McKenzie, for her calf, and for all the other cows in that barn."

The woods finally came into view, their sun-dappled clearing offering a moment of quiet relief. They found McKenzie resting where they had left her, a little girl was now sitting beside her, softly stroking her head. She wore a worried expression.

Rocco, Penny, and Sarge froze, afraid this might be someone from the farm to take McKenzie back with them, but the girl looked up with teary eyes. "Is she hurt? Can I help?"

Relieved, the three of them approached together and hurriedly tried to explain the situation the farm, the missing calves, and what the other mama cows had told them like a frantic game of charades. The little girl watched their animated gestures, her face shifting from confusion to understanding.

The girl stood, brushing the leaves from her skirt. "My name is Paige. I live up the road," the little girl said softly. Then, glancing at McKenzie, she asked, "Are you trying to tell me this cow ran away from that farm trying to find her baby?"

Rocco, Penny, and Sarge nodded eagerly, tails wagging as they sensed Paige beginning to understand. They continued their animated efforts, waving their paws, mimicking motor noises, making soft baby moo sounds, and pretending to drink from imaginary glasses. Their expressive faces and gestures told a story without words, and Paige watched closely, her brows furrowed in concentration as she pieced it together.

She replayed in her mind what she had just watched them act out for her—the truck, the baby calf, the milk—and her heart sank. A growing unease settled over her as the truth started to take shape. Her gaze fell on McKenzie, who looked back at her with an expression so full of sadness and longing that it seemed to confirm everything.

The realization hit her like a wave. "All my life, I thought the cows on that farm were happy," she said, her voice trembling. "I thought they made milk just because they were dairy cows—that it was just what they did. I had no idea they had to keep having babies to make milk or that they weren't allowed to raise their calves, that they don't have any choice." Tears welled in her eyes as she looked at McKenzie, her heart aching. "This isn't right. It's breaking my heart."

Paige felt overwhelmed by everything she had just learned but knew coming up with a solution was far too big to tackle on her own. "I'm going home to talk to my parents—we have to do something to help! We can't let this happen to McKenzie or any of the other mama cows on that farm. I'll be back as soon as I can, I promise!"

With a final, gentle pat on McKenzie's head, she turned and sprinted away, tears glistening in her eyes.

McKenzie watched her go, a flicker of hope growing in her chest. The kindness Paige, Rocco, Penny, and Sarge had shown her was unlike anything she had ever known. For the first time, McKenzie felt something she thought might be love, and it made her want to believe in the promise Paige had made.

At home, Paige wiped her tears and found her parents in the kitchen. Her voice trembling with urgency, she launched into a heartfelt explanation of what she had learned about the life of a cow on the farm and the scared, desperate mama cow she had just met in the woods.

"Did you know that cows don't magically produce milk just because they're 'dairy cows'?", she began passionately. "They make milk because they've just had a baby, the same way a human mother does. But on dairy farms, the calves are taken away from their mothers within hours or days after birth so people can drink the milk instead!"

Her parents exchanged startled glances, her mom's brow furrowed with concern. "We had no idea," her mom admitted quietly.

Paige's voice rose, filled with determination. "Isn't there something we can do? Now that we know what these mamas and calves go through, we can't just stand by and do nothing?"

Her dad sighed, his expression torn. "We'd like to help, but those cows belong to the farmer. We can't just take them because we don't agree with what is happening."

Paige looked horrified. "Belong to the farmer?" she repeated, her voice trembling. "McKenzie loves her baby so much that she chased a truck until she nearly collapsed—and she's just property to him? All of those cows are sweet, helpless creatures with feelings. They experience love, happiness, loneliness, and fear, just like dogs, cats, and people do. McKenzie is so smart, loving, and gentle. If you'd just come with me and meet her, you'd see. She needs our help—they all do!"

"She's right," her mom said gently, taking Paige's hand. "Cows are very intelligent and if given the chance, they are wonderful mothers that form very strong bonds with their babies. We can't just pretend we don't know what is happening to them and their calves after what Paige just told us."

Before her dad could respond, there was a quiet commotion at the kitchen door. He opened it to find McKenzie, Rocco, Penny, and Sarge standing there. They had followed Paige home, anxious to hear if she could help.

Seeing McKenzie, her head hanging low and tears glistening in her eyes, shattered any lingering doubts Paige's parents had. Her mom's face softened, and her dad let out a long sigh. They exchanged determined glances, their expressions resolute.

"We'll figure something out," her dad said firmly. "We need a plan—a good one—and then we need to talk to the farmer."

They sat down at the kitchen table, the weight of the moment pressing on them. Ideas began to flow as they talked about how they could help not just McKenzie and her calf, but other animals too.

"What if we built a sanctuary?" Paige's mom suggested, her voice growing more excited. "A safe place where animals could live free and happy, without fear."

The room lit up with energy as they realized how many lives they could save by creating such a haven. It would be a place where animals of all kinds could finally know what freedom, love, happiness, and dignity felt like.

"We can section off a large part of the pasture for the cows," her dad said, sketching a rough layout on the back of an envelope. "We'll need sturdy fencing to keep them safe."

"And what about food?" Paige's mom added thoughtfully. "We could dedicate more land to the garden for growing grass and vegetables for them. We could even support the sanctuary by selling some of what we grow at our own farmer's market!"

Paige's face lit up. "I can help raise money! We could invite people to visit the sanctuary and teach about the animals we rescue. If they hear their stories, they might want to help too!"

The family brainstormed late into the evening, their ideas coming together piece by piece. With every detail they added, it felt more and more like this was what they were meant to do all along.

Finally, they had a plan that felt right. But before they could bring it to life, they knew they had to talk to the farmer. After all, his agreement was crucial for much of their plan to work, at least in the beginning.

After a long day of planning and preparation, the family decided it was too late to do anything more. They sat down to eat a quick meal and agreed that tomorrow morning, first thing, they would go talk to the farmer.

As they wrapped up for the night in the soft glow of the kitchen, their hearts were full of hope. Anticipating an early start, they all headed to bed, eager to turn their dreams into reality.

Upstairs, Paige lay awake for a while, her mind buzzing with thoughts of the sanctuary and the animals they could help. Smiling to herself, she drifted off to sleep, imagining the sound of happy hooves and paws running free.

Downstairs, McKenzie was nestled safely near her new friends, Rocco, Penny, and Sarge. The trio curled up together beside her, drifting off to sleep almost immediately, their steady breathing blending with the peaceful quiet of the house.

Outside, the night was calm and still, with the stars shining brighter than ever as if they were rooting for the family's plan to succeed.

The next morning, as the sun rose, so did Paige's determination to make a difference. She rushed into the kitchen, eager to greet McKenzie, Rocco, Penny, and Sarge and ready to hit the road.

The family headed out to the truck, ready to make their way down to the farm and convince the farmer to agree to their plan. Rocco, Penny, and Sarge were just as eager and insisted on coming along and they happily piled into the back of the truck.

McKenzie stayed behind at the house, trusting her new-found family with her fate. She seemed content to wait, clearly in no hurry to return to the farm where her troubles had begun.

As they settled into the truck, the air was filled with a mix of excitement and nervous energy.

Paige glanced back at McKenzie, who was watching them from the safety of the house, her eyes calm and trusting. It was as if McKenzie knew this family was about to change her life—and maybe the lives of many others.

With a deep breath, Paige shifted her focus forward, holding tightly to the plan they had carefully crafted the night before. The truck rumbled to life, and they set off, ready to take their first step toward transforming countless lives.

When they arrived at the farm, the scene was a mix of early-morning calm and industrious activity. The farmer was finishing his chores near the big red barn, his face weathered and focused.

Paige's dad approached him with a friendly yet purposeful stride. "Excuse me, sir. We'd like to talk to you about McKenzie......and the other cows."

The farmer paused, leaning on his pitchfork. His expression shifted from curiosity to guardedness as Paige and her parents explained McKenzie's story—how she had chased after the truck carrying her baby, nearly collapsing from exhaustion, and how Paige had found her terrified and alone in the woods.

The farmer's eyes widened in surprise. "I never imagined a cow could understand enough to do something like that," he admitted, his voice filled with disbelief. "They're just... well, they're just cows. I've never really stopped to think about how they might feel about what happens here." He shifted uncomfortably, rubbing the back of his neck. "But I've got a business to run, and my family depends on the money we make from selling milk."

Paige's mom stepped forward, her voice steady but kind. "We understand that, and we have a proposal for you. We're starting an animal sanctuary on our land—a place where calves can live if they can't stay here, and where older cows can retire once they're done producing milk."

Her dad nodded. "We'd also like to volunteer our help around your farm if you'll let us. You won't need to hire as many farmhands, which could save you money. We're willing to work hard to make this a partnership that benefits everyone—especially the animals."

The farmer hesitated, he looked directly at Paige, his expression softening, and said, "You seem like the mastermind behind this. Am I right? Why are you so set on helping these animals?"

Paige stepped forward, her voice unwavering. "Because they deserve better. McKenzie chased that truck because she loved her baby. She doesn't see herself or her calf as property—and neither do we. We can make a difference, starting with her and her calf but we can't do it without your help."

Hearing McKenzie's story was beginning to change the way the farmer thought about his animals. He had always seen them as part of the business, but now, he found himself wondering if there was more to their lives than he had allowed himself to see. The offer of free help on the farm didn't hurt either, but it was the earnestness in Paige's voice that struck a chord.

The farmer hesitated, his gaze drifting toward the barn. Finally, he sighed, his voice softening. "All right," he said. "I'll agree on a trial basis. I'll also make a promise to do better by these cows—they deserve more than small stalls and lonely nights. Heck, I'll take a good look at how I can improve the quality of life for all the animals on this farm."

He turned back to Paige, a faint smile tugging at the corners of his mouth. "Maybe you can help me with some ideas when you come down here to volunteer?"

Paige's face lit up, her heart swelling with gratitude. "Absolutely!" she replied eagerly. The chance to help even more animals and be part of meaningful change at the farm filled her with hope.

Just then, the farmer's phone rang, cutting through the moment. Mumbling an apology, he stepped aside to take the call. Moments later, he returned, his face drawn with worry.

The Dad asked the farmer if everything was alright, star-
tling him back from his frustrated thoughts.

The farmer turned to them and said, "That was the driver
of the truck carrying the baby calf you're looking for, along
with a few other newborns. The truck has broken down on
its way out of town and was stranded up the road, and the
driver can't get it running."

He paused, then added, "If you can get that truck running
again and back on schedule, I'll have the calves dropped
off at your sanctuary before the driver heads out of town,
they can be your first residents—oh, and the runaway cow
can go too."

Paige bristled at the farmer's words, biting her tongue as
he referred to McKenzie as "the runaway cow." Honestly,
she thought indignantly, her name is McKenzie! But with
one more important question to ask, she decided now
wasn't the time to correct him. Instead, she took a deep
breath, flashed him a bright smile, and said, "Thank you!
But... Do you think I could ask you for one more thing?"

The farmer let out a good-natured chuckle, tipping his hat back slightly. "Well now, I guess I should have known I wouldn't get off that easy, all right, what's this 'one more thing'?"

Paige took a breath, her heart racing with hope. "Would you let us bring the babies down to visit their mamas here, maybe when they're out in the pasture grazing? Their bond is so important and it's heartbreaking to know they will be so close but never get to see each other."

The farmer scratched his chin thoughtfully, his brow furrowed. After a moment, he nodded. "You drive a hard bargain, little lady. How's this? So long as it doesn't mean any extra work for me, and it doesn't disrupt the schedule here at the farm, you can bring the calves for visits whenever you want." Paige's face lit up. It took everything in her not to jump up and down with excitement.

Her parents thanked the farmer warmly, shook his hand, and promised to head straight out to help the stranded truck driver. They piled back into the truck, hearts full of hope, and left the farm before the farmer changed his mind.

When they got home, McKenzie was waiting in the front yard, her big brown eyes fixed on the approaching truck. Paige quickly scrambled out and ran to her side, gently pressing her forehead against McKenzie's. "You'll see your baby soon," she whispered. McKenzie closed her eyes and let out a deep, relieved breath.

Paige's dad set out to help the stranded truck driver, while the rest of the family started to explain to McKenzie everything they had arranged with the farmer. She would get to see her mama cow friends again, she would never have to return to the life of a dairy cow, and the other calves would also be reunited with their mothers. But nothing could compare to the news that her baby would soon be by her side again.

Overwhelmed with gratitude, McKenzie gently wrapped her large head around Paige's shoulders in a tender, heartfelt cow hug. Paige hugged her back, feeling the deep connection between them. Rocco, Penny, and Sarge couldn't hold back their enthusiasm and piled into the hug, wagging their tails furiously. In that moment, it felt like love and hope had found a way to heal everything.

Not long after Paige's dad got the broken-down truck running again, it pulled into their driveway to make a very special delivery. McKenzie stood anxiously near the fence, her eyes fixed on the trailer, her body tense with anticipation.

When the gate opened, a tiny calf stepped out, his wide, curious eyes scanning his new surroundings, soft distressed cries escaping from him. It was McKenzie's baby. She rushed to him, letting out a soft, relieved moo as she tenderly groomed his ears. He leaned into her side, nuzzling her with pure affection, his small cries now quieted in the comfort of her presence.

The reunion was nothing short of magical, bringing tears to everyone's eyes. Watching McKenzie and her calf together was a powerful reminder of why Paige and her family had chosen this path—to create a world where love and freedom replaced fear and separation.

McKenzie, as if understanding her role as the sanctuary's first ambassador, gently nuzzled the other calves, offering them a sense of reassurance she let them know that they'd be seeing their mothers the next day too.

Meanwhile, the family worked tirelessly to be as prepared as possible to safely care for their very first guests. With acres of land surrounding their home, they felt grateful to have the space to embrace this new chapter in their lives.

Paige and her parents worked late into the evening, securing fences, gathering supplies from the feed store, and setting up a cozy temporary shelter for their very first guests. The sanctuary was already becoming a place where hope took root, one step at a time.

In the days, weeks, and months that followed, the sanctuary's vision grew larger and more ambitious. The family worked closely with veterinarians and animal rescue experts to design accommodations and provide care that met the unique needs of every animal they welcomed.

They built expansive enclosures and warm and cozy barns. They expanded the gardens to grow enough nutritious food, ensuring their sanctuary residents would have healthy meals.

As the sanctuary flourished, they expanded their efforts, creating a rehabilitation center for injured or sick animals and launching a foster and adoption program, connecting rescued animals with loving homes.

Inspired by McKenzie's journey and the lessons it taught them, Paige's family embraced a fully plant-based, dairy-free lifestyle. They realized that aligning their daily choices with their values of compassion and empathy was just as important as saving the animals themselves. Together, they were building not just a sanctuary for animals, but a life rooted in kindness and integrity.

Healing
Haven
Adopt
Me

Over time, the sanctuary blossomed into a legendary haven of compassion, known for giving animals a second chance at life. It became a beacon of hope, welcoming a growing family of rescued animals: chickens, sheep, goats, pigs, horses, and of course, cows, and even cats and dogs. Their rescue did not discriminate, all those in need were welcome.

McKenzie and her son, who was eventually named Cain, naturally embraced their roles as the sanctuary's unofficial welcoming committee. Having endured fear and heartbreak themselves, they seemed to instinctively understand the needs of the new arrivals. With gentle nuzzles, loving care, and patience, they offered each newcomer a sense of safety, love, and belonging, ensuring every animal felt valued and cherished from the moment they arrived.

Rocco, Penny, and Sarge visited the sanctuary every day, their joyful energy lighting up the fields. They bounded through the gates, eager to play with their new friends, their wagging tails a symbol of the sanctuary's warmth. Each in their own way, the trio's adventurous spirit, gentle empathy, and steady companionship became a vital part of the sanctuary's heart, helping to create a place where every creature could thrive.

Paige often stood at the edge of the pasture, watching McKenzie and Cain graze peacefully side by side in the tall, sunlit grass. They were the ones who had started it all, the spark that ignited an epic mission. On most days, the farmer allowed the mama cows from his farm to join them, reuniting with their calves under the open sky for much-needed moments of connection. Even he had come to realize that treating these sentient beings with care and respect, rather than seeing them as mere property, brought an unexpected sense of fulfillment.

Though there was still much work ahead—rescuing more animals, improving the farm, and expanding the sanctuary—Paige felt a deep sense of purpose. She was happier than she could ever remember being. She knew she was doing exactly what she was put on this earth to do, creating a kinder world for animals, one rescued soul at a time.